Craig Soapy

Karen Smart

Terry Flynn

Fatima Patel

Lily Wongsam

Paul Dimbley

# THIS IS BOB WILSON

He wrote this story
and drew the pictures.

He lives in the Derbyshire countryside in a house which he designed and built himself from an old cowshed. He has three grown-up children and nine grandchildren. When he was young he wanted to be a pop star, and he started to write songs. He became an art teacher and wrote plays and musicals, and shows for television and radio. Then he began to write and illustrate stories for children. He is the author of the *Stanley Bagshaw* picture books and the best-selling *Ging Gang Goolie, It's an Alien!*

First published 2000 by Macmillan Children's Books
a division of Macmillan Publishers Limited
20 New Wharf Road, London N1 9RR
Basingstoke and Oxford
www.panmacmillan.com

Associated companies throughout the world

ISBN 0 330 37091 X

Copyright © Bob Wilson 2000

579864

A CIP catalogue record for this book is available from
the British Library.

Printed and bound in Great Britain by Mackays of Chatham plc, Kent

Visit Bob Wilson's website at www.planetbob.co.uk

written and illustrated by
Bob Wilson

MACMILLAN CHILDREN'S BOOKS

# Here are some of the school staff ...

Mr C Warrilow BSc MEd

Miss Twigg

Mr Manley

Mr Boggis

Mrs York

Mr Lamp-Williams

Miss Gaters

Mrs Jellie

Norman Loops

Janice

Mrs Brazil

For Ami, Thomas, Elias,
Matilda, Reuben, Alexander,
Marius, Lucien and Babik

# THIS IS FREDDIE STANTON

He's incredibly fit and athletic.
He's also quiet, reserved and modest.

Not like Mr Manley.
Mr Manley is a new teacher at our
school. At the start of term he came
into the classroom and introduced
himself to Miss Twigg.

Manley's the name. But
you, my dear, may call
me Bernard.

Mr Manley is an unusual sort of teacher. For example, at Parents' Evening our class teacher, Miss Twigg, talked about how well we were doing with our work.

But Mr Manley didn't talk about our work. He talked about himself.

Mr Manley has also got what Miss Twigg calls an "over-inflated ego". (I think she means that he's a know-all.) He certainly knows all about football.

But, being new to the school, he didn't know about *our* football team. Which is why, when he read the notice on the board in the entrance hall he got quite a surprise.

It was last term's results.

# Pump Street Primary School
## Head teacher: Mr C. Warrilow

Pump Street
Burston-on-Tweddle
Derbyshire
DE6 2GP

Tel: (01335) 324632

## LOWER JUNIORS' FOOTBALL RESULTS
## AUTUMN TERM

| | | | |
|---|---|---|---|
| Pike Hall Juniors: | 6 | Pump Street: | 0 |
| Waterhouses Middle: | 4 | Pump Street: | 2 |
| Pump Street: | 0 | St Modwen's: | 11 |
| Dove First School: | 7 | Pump Street: | 1 |
| Pump Street: | 2 | Henry Prince C of E: | 13 |
| Sacred Heart: | 9 | Pump Street: | 0 |
| Pump Street: | 1 | Norbury Primary: | 5 |
| St Mildred's: | 37 | Pump Street: | 0 |

## CURRENT LEAGUE POSITIONS

| | Played | Won | Drawn | Lost | Points |
|---|---|---|---|---|---|
| St Mildred's | 8 | 8 | 0 | 0 | 24 |
| Henry Prince | 7 | 4 | 2 | 1 | 14 |
| Dove First | 8 | 4 | 2 | 2 | 14 |
| Pike Hall | 8 | 3 | 3 | 2 | 12 |
| Waterhouses | 7 | 3 | 3 | 1 | 12 |
| St Modwen's | 8 | 3 | 2 | 3 | 11 |
| Norbury | 7 | 2 | 3 | 2 | 9 |
| Sacred Heart | 7 | 3 | 0 | 4 | 9 |
| Pump Street | 8 | 0 | 0 | 8 | 0 |

And a letter from Miss Twigg which said

"Yes," said Miss Twigg. "But they did do their best, they did play fair and they didn't *ever* give up."

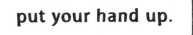

Miss Twigg smiled and said,

And Mr Manley
smiled and said . . .

Girls don't play football, my dear. Football is a man's game.

Karen Smart said,

Actually, sir, girls do play football.

Not in MY team they don't!

said Mr Manley.

Then he turned to the boys and said,
"Right, lads."

Training sessions . . . every
Monday . . . after school . . .
four till six. Be there.

And all the boys said, "Yes, sir!" and
"Sure thing!" and "You bet".
Except for Freddie Stanton who said,
"Sorry, sir. I can't come. Not on
Mondays."

I do dancing on
Mondays.

"Dancing?" said Mr Manley.

Karen Smart said,

"Leave it, Karen," said Miss Twigg.
"Let me deal with this. Mr Manley, I'd
like a word in private."
"Very well," said Mr Manley.
So Miss Twigg and Mr Manley went
out into the corridor so that they could
talk in private.

Miss Twigg said,

Freddie is shaping up to be a very good goalkeeper. He's agile and athletic — and regular attendance at my dance class has made him really fit. I don't see why—

"Nonsense," said Mr Manley. "Footballers have to be strong and fearless and brave. They have to learn to do hard, skilful things.
All that dancers do is prance and pose and jig up and down to music. I'm not having an airy-fairy dancer in my team. And as far as I'm concerned," he said, "that's the end of the matter!"
BUT IT WASN'T.
Because, as far as Miss Twigg was concerned . . .
IT WAS JUST THE START OF IT!

# EVERY MONDAY AFTER SCHOOL

the boys were out on the field practising hard, skilful footballing things like ball control . . .

and shooting

and fearlessly throwing themselves at the ball in a brave attempt to score.

# WHILE IN THE HALL

Freddie Stanton and the girls were
messing about doing "airy-fairy"
dancing things like prancing

and posing

and jigging up and down to music.

Sometimes the boys would be given a lecture on football tactics.
(Mr Manley was an expert on tactics.)

**Tactics are the cunning ways by which you may gain advantage over your opponent.**

One of his tactics was called

TAKING A DIVE

**If you fall over, act as if you've been tripped up. With luck you'll get a penalty.**

When Rashid suggested that this tactic was not very sporting, Mr Manley said,

Mr Manley was very keen on winning. Sometimes he drew complicated diagrams on the board. He called this planning a winning strategy.
(Mr Manley was an expert on strategy.)

His favourite strategy was called

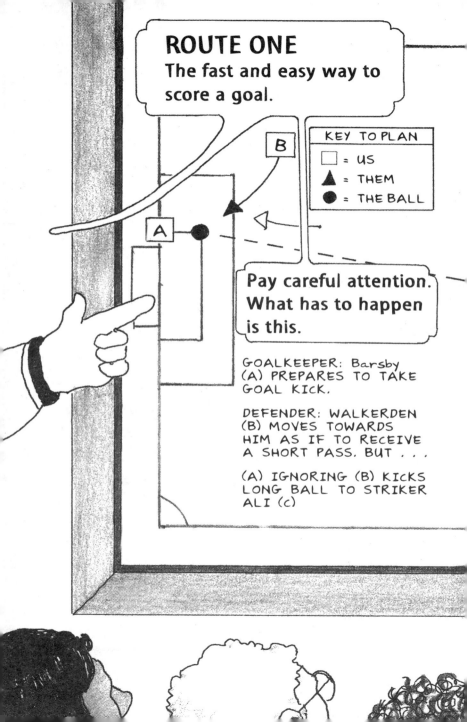

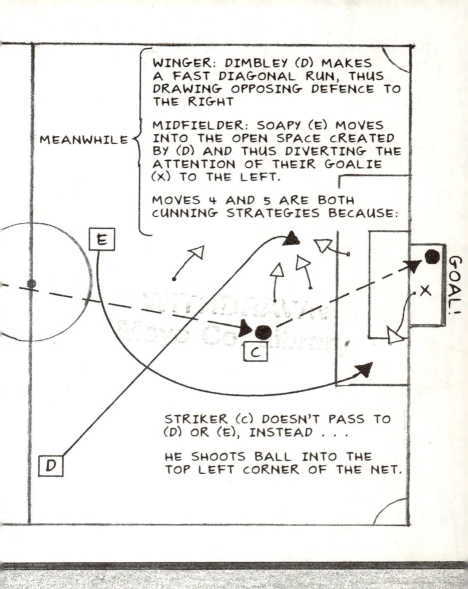

WINGER: DIMBLEY (D) MAKES A FAST DIAGONAL RUN, THUS DRAWING OPPOSING DEFENCE TO THE RIGHT

MEANWHILE {

MIDFIELDER: SOAPY (E) MOVES INTO THE OPEN SPACE CREATED BY (D) AND THUS DIVERTING THE ATTENTION OF THEIR GOALIE (X) TO THE LEFT.

MOVES 4 AND 5 ARE BOTH CUNNING STRATEGIES BECAUSE:

GOAL!

STRIKER (c) DOESN'T PASS TO (D) OR (E), INSTEAD . . .

HE SHOOTS BALL INTO THE TOP LEFT CORNER OF THE NET.

This is what was supposed to happen. But what *usually* happened was

Barry Barsby (Goalkeeper) is still getting changed because (as usual) he's turned up late.

A

A

So Rashid Ali (c) takes the kick instead. He's meant to kick the ball to the striker but he can't because he's the striker so instead ...

SO

B

he passes the ball to Mark Walkerden (B).

B

C

D

MY BALL!

MY BALL!

E

But Mark doesn't realise that the ball is behind him because he's too busy looking at a really big slug he's just found in the grass by his feet.

E

**Walkerden, you idiot! Don't just stand there like a love-struck fairy. Kick the thing!**

At half-time Mr Manley always went to great pains to explain exactly what we needed to do to win the game.

**Stop pratting about like a bunch of brainless sheep!**

But despite Mr Manley's efforts, the result was always the same . . . *we lost*. He decided to try a new strategy. It was called

threats

and promises.

But the boys were getting tired of being shouted at. And these particular threats and promises had no effect because . . .

some of the boys had already joined the
dancing class.

It's good fun. You
should try it.

Others simply seemed to have lost
interest in the game.

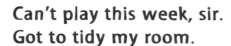

Can't play this week, sir.
Got to tidy my room.

Lately Mr Manley had been having a
job to raise the eleven players for a
team.
There was certainly never anyone sitting
on his subs bench. And this was causing
him some concern because the last game
of the season was against the best team
in the league.

"St Mildred's?" said Miss Twigg when she saw the team sheet. "Well I never."

And then she smiled.

But Mr Manley overheard what she said and he wasn't very pleased.
He said, "All right. That's enough of that."

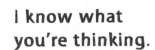

## BUT HE DIDN'T

He thought that Miss Twigg was looking forward to seeing his team get beaten. He thought she was being a bad sport.

## BUT SHE WASN'T

What she was looking forward to was seeing Mr Manley's face when he saw the St Mildred's football team.
Because there was something about the St Mildred's football team that was *rather unusual*.
And she had just smiled because she had just thought of

## A PLAN!

A cunning strategy by means of which I may defeat the enemy.

## THE FOLLOWING DAY

Miss Twigg put her plan into action.
In the morning she had a quiet word
with Barry Barsby.

In the afternoon she had a quiet word
with Freddie Stanton.

And in the evening, after
everybody had gone home,
she did a bit of photocopying.

and we were all very excited. But the kick off wasn't until 4 o'clock. First we had to do ordinary lessons. Some people found it hard to concentrate.

When at last the bell went for end of school we all trooped round to the football field singing the Earwig song.

The St Mildred's supporters were already there. And they'd made a big banner.

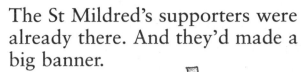

## St Mildred's are the best

So we made one too.

Meanwhile

# IN THE CHANGING ROOM

Mr Manley was talking to Rashid Ali, our team captain. It was a tactical talk.

These St Mildred's lads will be expecting to win. They'll likely be over-confident. And they'll be expecting us to be cautious and defensive.

He told Rashid the plan.

But I shall outwit them because I've a plan.

Go out there and WIN!

"We'll do our best, sir," said Rashid. Then he ran out onto the field to tell the others Mr Manley's plan.

Miss Twigg was having a word with the referee.

Mr Manley was still in the changing room when the referee came in.
"Ah, ref," said Mr Manley. "I expect you'll be wanting our team sheet."
But the ref had just come in to go to the toilet. He'd already got the Pump Street team sheet.

A nice young lady gave it to me.

A nice young lady?

Out on the field the team were having their photograph taken.
At least *most* of them were.

Where's Barsby?

"Haven't seen him, sir," said Rashid Ali. "Perhaps he's been kidnapped by alien space monsters," said Paul Dimbley. "Actually, Mr Manley, I asked Barry to run me a little errand," said Miss Twigg.

"You silly woman!" said Mr Manley.
"He'll be late. He's always late."
Miss Twigg smiled and said, "Perhaps
you should have a word with the
referee."
The ref was at the other end of the
pitch. And when Mr Manley got there
he discovered the thing that was *rather
unusual* about the St Mildred's football
team.

"That's right," said the referee. "And they're the best team in the league."
Mr Manley went very quiet.
Then all of a sudden he said, "I've got it! That's it! We've got no goalie. We can't play them anyway."
The ref didn't understand.
"He's not turned up," said Mr Manley. "You'll have to abandon the match."
But the ref still didn't understand. He said, "I don't see the problem. Why can't you play your substitute goalie?"

"Because we haven't got a substitute goalie," said Mr Manley.

**According to this team sheet you have.**

**Excuse me, Mr Manley?**

said Miss Twigg.

Mr Manley protested, "He's not a
footballer. He's a dancer!"
But the referee said, "What of it?"
Freddie Stanton's name was on the team
sheet so Freddie would have to play.
And it was time to start the match.
So we took up our positions according
to Mr Manley's plan.
But just as we were about to kick
off . . .

Mr Manley ran onto the pitch.

Rashid looked at Mr Manley's new plan and said,

To which Mr Manley replied, "Football isn't always about winning. Sometimes it's about not losing."

"No, sir," said Rashid.
"Well then," said Mr Manley. "Just do as you're told!"

Rashid is a good boy, who always does as he's told, so he said, "We'll do what we can, sir."
Then ran back to the others to show them the new plan.

It was a rather unusual plan. We were now going for . . .

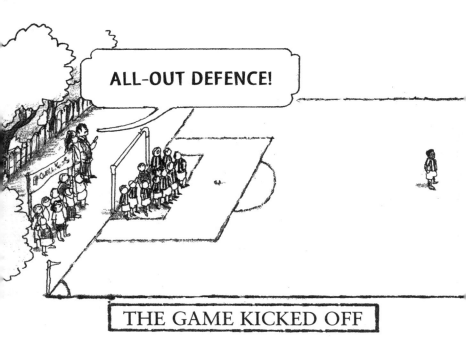

ALL-OUT DEFENCE!

## THE GAME KICKED OFF

and St Mildred's immediately went onto
the attack. They passed and dribbled,
and took the ball to the
by-line; they sent in high crosses and
low crosses. They had free kicks and
headers and hundreds of hard low shots
but they just couldn't find a way round
the Pump Street defensive wall.
Freddie never had to make a save.
*He never even got to touch the ball.*

## AT HALF-TIME

the score was still nil-nil.
"I'm a tactical genius," said Mr Manley.
"You're mean and unsporting, and you're
spoiling the game," said Miss Twigg.
Mr Manley didn't care. He said his
strategy was working.
He said,

I'm more than a match
for a load of schoolgirls.

BUT HE SPOKE
TOO SOON!

Because five minutes before the end of the game, St Mildred's won a corner.

MR MANLEY WASN'T WORRIED
They'd had lots of corners already and they'd all come to nothing. He thought that as long as his lads did as they were told he'd got nothing to worry about.

BUT HE WAS WRONG.
Because this time the corner was being taken by Yasmin Bibi. And not only did Yasmin Bibi have an immensely powerful left foot, she also had . . .

A PLAN!

A cunning plan by which I may gain an advantage over my opponent.

Or in other words,
A REALLY SNEAKY TRICK!

was quite simple.

For not only was Yasmin St Mildred's best player, she was also Rashid Ali's cousin. And she knew that Rashid was a good boy who *always* did as he was told.

So when Yasmin took the corner she didn't do what everyone expected her to do. She didn't cross the ball hard and high into the goal mouth.

She simply lobbed it gently towards Rashid and said,

Here, Rashid, catch.

And Rashid, who always did as he was told,

caught it.

**OH NO!**

It was a penalty.
Yasmin Bibi smiled. Yasmin always took
the penalties for St Mildred's.
And she *never* missed. And today the
only thing standing between her and a
certain goal was . . . .

little Freddie Stanton.

The St Mildred's supporters started to sing.

# Eee-Ay . . .
# addi . . . oh
## We're going to score
## A GOAL!

So we started singing too.

Then the ref blew his whistle. It was
time for the kick.
The crowd went very quiet.
Yasmin Bibi strode confidently up to the
ball . . . and gave it an almighty thump.

It was heading for the top corner. A
certain goal, no doubt about it.
Freddie just stood there watching it,
watching the flight of the ball. And then
he just . . .

leapt into the air and caught it.

Freddie had saved the penalty. What's more, there was just one minute to go to the final whistle and we still weren't losing!

BUT THE BEST WAS YET TO COME!

Because Freddie had noticed that the St Mildred's goalie was standing a long way off her goal-line.
And decided to do something about it.

"What on earth does Stanton think he's doing?" said Mr Manley.

"Well," said Miss Twigg.

"What Freddie is doing is what we 'airy-fairy dancers' call a pirouette, followed by an arabesque, followed by a leap,"

The ref blew the final whistle.
We could hardly believe it.

## WE WON THE MATCH!

And Freddie was our hero.

It was Barry Barsby.

I'm not too early am I, Miss?

"No, Barry," said Miss Twigg. "You're not too early. In fact,"

Your timing was perfect!

Mr Warrilow, the head teacher, congratulated the team on their great sporting achievement.
"Football," he said, "is a team game. However,"

(Mr Manley stood up.)

(Mr Manley sat down again.)

"Freddie, I'm very proud of you," said Mr Warrilow.

"Not really, sir," said Freddie.

Mr Warrilow was so moved by the modesty of Freddie's reply that he felt the need to make a speech about it. He finished his speech by saying,

And we did.

The dance show was a huge success.
The audience loved the "Spot-the-Ball
Ballet" and the "Corner-kick Can-can".
When the Lower Juniors danced the
"One-nil Victory Polka" everyone
cheered.
But the dance we enjoyed most of
all was the "Dance of the Sugar Plum
Full-back", performed by none other
than . . .

# Mr Bernard Manley!

THE END

# MONICA'S MONSTER

Miss Twigg likes animals. But when Monica
brings little Samantha to school and says

Please, Miss,
would you like to see
my pet?

Miss Twigg says

NO!

# RASHID'S RESCUE

Miss Twigg says

If all my class were like Rashid my life would be free of stress.

But when she takes the children on a factory visit something happens to change her mind.

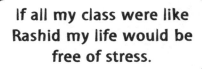

I nearly get glooped and grundled by a Galvanised Gasket Gargler!

# PUMP STREET PRIMARY
## titles available from Macmillan

The prices shown below are correct at the time of going to press. However, Macmillan Publishers reserve the right to show new retail prices on covers which may differ from those previously advertised.

| | | |
|---|---|---|
| Football Fred | 0 330 37091 X | £3.50 |
| Monica's Monster | 0 330 37093 6 | £3.50 |
| Rashid's Rescue | 0 330 37095 2 | £3.50 |
| Lucky Lily | 0 330 39818 0 | £3.99 |
| Daring Dan | 0 330 39819 9 | £3.99 |

All Macmillan titles can be ordered at your local bookshop or are available by post from:

**Book Service by Post**
**PO Box 29, Douglas, Isle of Man IM99 1BQ**

Credit cards accepted. For details:
Telephone: 01624 675137
Fax: 01624 670923
E-mail: bookshop@enterprise.net

**Free postage and packing in the UK.**
Overseas customers: add £1 per book (paperback)
and £3 per book (hardback)